Lend ME YOUR *Eyes*

ASHTON MORGAN

Lend Me Your Eyes

Lend ME YOUR Eyes

ASHTON MORGAN

Lend Me Your Eyes

Ashton Morgan

This book you're reading is a work of fiction. Characters, places, events, and names are the product of this author's imagination. Any resemblance to other events, other locations, or other persons, living or dead, is coincidental.

First Edition. Originally published in e-book and paperback format by Ashton Morgan in February 2024.

Summary:
What happens, after death? Follow Bellamy and Loralai into their magical adventure into what happens after we're gone. The journey, the heartbreak, and the relief.

ASIN: B0CTY9J5QL (ebook)
ISBN: (paperback)
BN: 979-8878760768 (paperback)
ISBN: 979-8-3305-1457-1 (Ingram ebook)
ISBN: 979-8-3305-1456-4 (Ingram Paperback)

TABLE OF CONTENTS

I   11

II   15

III   20

IV   26

V   31

VI   39

VII   43

VIII   48

IX   54

X   59

ADDENDUM   65

Lend Me Your Eyes

Ashton Morgan

9

For the guideless.

Lend Me Your Eyes

I

BELLAMY SQUINTED INTO THE OVERHEAD light, holding a hand above his head and looking around. The ground was soft beneath his feet as he took a step forward. Ahead lay a wrought iron arch, stuck out of the ground, suggesting that someone had come by with a building plan and abandoned it after constructing the entryway. Only a rusted gate remained, half hanging off its hinges.

Tall cedar trees stretched toward the sky, bent in and leaning over the small clearing he stood in. The soft scent of wildflowers crept over the distant hillside, the surrounding wood quiet in anticipation. Golden pine needles made a pathway fit for a fairytale.

This was no fantasy.

Bellamy continued onward, running his hand along the rough metal as he passed, turning toward the hillside. Soft stalks of wheat waved with the gentle breeze, combing through the pink clouds overhead. Thunderless lightning struck above, engulfing the clouds he never would have known were there. Slowly, he crossed the threshold. Held his breath. And, when nothing came, he blew out all the air in his lungs.

A moon rose overhead, large and observant. A late afternoon breeze drifted past, lifting his unzipped jacket off his waist. Bellamy put his hands in his pockets.

Lightning struck again, distantly. The clouds turned pink, wounded, swirling overhead in colours that mocked the sunset. Sun-dried grass sprung back to life beneath his feet, turning brown again when he stepped away.

Woods lined the path ahead of him, deep and foreboding. Welcoming, beckoning. Bellamy took a step backward.

He shook his head, waiting for the dream to end.

When it didn't, he steeled himself, staring back at the wheat stalks waving him onward, and pressed forward.

The trees leaned inward overtop of him, shielding him from the stars above, listening for the secrets that still lingered on his skin, that he whispered to the Earth. He toed the ground ahead of him tentatively, waiting for something to spring out of the darkness. It didn't.

Flowers bloomed under the starlight, turning to gaze up at him as he passed, a crowd parting around a godly figure passing through a mortal land; ineffable and divine. They faced forward again when he'd gone too far, turning, mirroring resolute statues, tiny soldiers guarding the path backward should he choose to turn around.

The sunset burned hot colours through the trees, casting pink and golden light down to the ground, little pools of light dancing on the forest floor. Bellamy stepped over them as if they were alive, frowning at his own silliness. Small orbs of light drifted up from the ground reminiscent of fireflies, floating softly through the air with the intimate knowledge of the insects, of what it meant to burn, glowing fainter as they rose before disappearing altogether. Rise, turn, repeat.

As the sun sank below the horizon line, they became the only consistent light, igniting the path in a dozen tiny flames, hanging off the grass and ferns like iron lanterns.

Nightfall soaked into the air around him, cloying in its heaviness. Bellamy wringed his hands, stopping only to feel the hair on the back of his neck rise, the mark of a lover had running a hand down his spine. *Stay,* they'd say. *Stay the night.*

Bellamy shuddered, huffing a breath of hot air into the cold. He ran his hands down his arms, content despite the frost that had begun to cover the ground. He dismissed the thought, and the path was again clear.

A voice lilted from behind, the flowers coming to attention around him. The whole world tipped one way, swaying, gripping the air by its throat, halting everything else. Nothing clear came of it, uttering a wordless feeling, a lilting tune. *Come. Stay.*

It was haunting. It was enchanting.

Bellamy turned to face the darkness and found only absence, as darkness might describe. Still, the charm persisted. Nothing had ever sounded so sweet, no better idea had ever been uttered. A melody twirling in the air he wished to make into song.

A sound cut through the air from the opposite direction. A sound so clear, so pristine, he should have recognized where it was from the second he heard it. Its familiarity beckoned him. It crawled inside his head, burning the edges of his thoughts away, growing roots among his memories. He knew, he knew. He needed to know.

The darkness spoke that enchanting language again, promising every good thing any mortal could crown as ambition. Every hunger, every wish.

Bellamy took a step back, and then another, and another. The darkness grew louder, echoing inside his head, calling out to every deep dark desire he'd shoved down and hoped to forget.

The darkness gave form to something wicked, crawling from the shadows. A litany, a seductress, speaking in a tone he should have known.

Icy water trickled down his spine, freezing him in place. He felt his fingers go numb, tingling with pinpricks of ice he was helpless to shake. *Move,* he urged his feet, stagnant and planted on the ground. *Move.*

The shadows grew closer. The small, golden lights blinking out under the oppressive darkness. Flowers turned gray the closer the shadows drew, soaking up every colour, wilting and disappearing into dust. The darkness seeped inward and the trees leaned away. Bellamy managed a step back, turning on his heel and running through the pine-needle path before him.

His choices might have been made for him, but they were still his.

The darkness surged forward, chasing him on the trail, whispering promises like caresses. The pinpricks of light aloft him winked out as darkness closed in from all sides, the evening sky above pounding down with crushing force.

The path ended abruptly as Bellamy stumbled into a clearing, open and wide. The darkness remained at the forest line, contained and dormant, waiting to embrace him should he change his mind. He wondered if the weight of its promise would be crushing or revered. He hoped to never know.

A moon sat against the sky distantly, overly huge and melting into the waterfall of a faraway cliff, the water turning a milky golden colour, glowing all the way down to where it crashed below. A house stood beside it. Old, and full of memories.

A voice chimed from behind him, clear as a bell. 'There you are,' it said.

He turned, finding a girl with dark hair and darker eyes stalking up to him, gazing with the recollection of an old friend. She checked a watch at her side, chain dangling from a pocket he couldn't see. 'I was wondering when you'd get here.'

II

HE BLINKED, AND THE DARKNESS cleared from his vision.

Ice curled through the air, dancing on the wind around him. A horn blew in the distance.

Moonlight shown on the frosted ground, glittering on the frozen Earth. Frost glinted silver, dew frozen on curled ferns, the land whispered to itself in hushed tones. Maybe now he might learn to listen.

The horn blew again, closer. A bright light glowed distantly, white and the size of a pin. The clearing opened up around him, snow covering the ground. The forest disappeared, leaving him alone in the icy light.

Bellamy blew out a breath, watched it frost midair. The light drew nearer, pushing its way toward him, impossible to ignore. The horn thundered again, and the ground rumbled in response. Stagnancy filled the air in between, the horn booming faster, quicker, desperation whining like an afterthought.

He stepped forward, tripping over something stuck out of the ground, kicking it as though it could have reached up and grabbed at his ankles. He tumbled forward, palms stuck out in front of him. Metal bit into his hands, the force of the landing singing up through his bones. He pushed to his knees, wrinkling his nose at the smell of smoke that filled the air, frowning as he turned back to face the light.

The horn sounded again, thunderous and impatient; a warning, an accompaniment. The ground shook feverishly, jaunting him back and forth. Snow fell off the metal on the ground, revealing tracks under his hands. The wooden boards beneath him promised splinters as he jumped to his feet, nerves rooting his body in place. The horn screamed again, the sound shuddering between his ears, drowning out every other outcome. Desperate, one of them would have their way.

He stepped off the rails and took a step back. The train barreled closer, unrelenting. He took another step back, putting his back to the train, forcing his feet to move. One step, two, forward and farther, the train closing the distance between them all the while.

He sidestepped, putting more distance between the tracks as he ran from the train, feeling the light on his back, a watchful eye.

The dark sky pressed down against him, heavy with prospect, leaning forward in its seat to get a better view. The horn blew again, so loud it at first appeared soundless, rattling him down to his marrow.

The dark whispered cold secrets against his cheek, running bitter hands up the length of his arms.

The train rumbled past, breaks screeching as someone familiar cried out.

'Come on!' She called, hanging out the window. Her hair haloed around her face for an instant before whipping back and around. Moonlight glinted above, casting light onto the top of her head. Bellamy watched as the train slowed, as the iron rails turned red hot beneath it, sparks flying up and around, golden fireworks splintering into the Earth.

He turned back to the window, and she was gone. His pace drifted to a jog, slowing as she appeared in the space between cars. 'Let's go!' She extended her arm.

Bellamy held his breath, pushed it down into his stomach. Stared ahead at the endless tracks, watching for a moment as his breath again hung in the cold air. The dusk shoved itself around him, cloying. He swallowed. Decided. He picked up his pace, casting all judgment aside, and took her hand.

BELLAMY TURNED ABOUT IN THE small cabin space of the train car, letting go of her hand once he steadied himself, and turned and look out the window.

The train pressed through the snow never once slowing. Pressed fast enough that there might have been no snow at all.

He turned back to her, finding himself alone in the small cabin. A door rested on the other wall beside where he'd come in. He pulled back the handle, the door sliding into the wall.

A dozen people sat in their seats, unamused and bored, as though the train had not slowed down enough so that he might jump inside.

He gazed at them as he passed, paying him no mind, faces a fog in his memory, blurring the minute he inspected them too closely, each of them a moment long ago and forgotten. He passed a blonde woman with otherwise kind eyes, a book in her lap and a small scar on her lip.

A man with polished shoes and mussed hair, staring out the window. A half-finished crossword held open in one hand, his other smeared with ink. He had no pen.

An old lady with a head scarf. A young boy with a worn, stuffed dog.

His chest grew tight, his arms aching to wrap around the strangers that lined the seats of the car, the strangers whose names he did not know. Bellamy took a shuddering breath, a coldness slipping over his shoulders with the weight of a blanket, gripping him by the arms and directing him somewhere new.

Something tapped on the window gently, scraping down the frosted glass like knives. *Tap, tap.* Bellamy looked toward the direction it came from, seeing nothing through the hazy, frosted window. *Tap, scratch.*

No one around him appeared bothered by the noise, seemed to notice. He cast another glance to the window, deciding he ought not pay it any mind either.

He cast around warily for an open seat. One near an old man who probably shouldn't have been smoking, puffing smog so thick it he mocked the train he rode on.

One near a young girl and her mother, talking animatedly about dinosaurs.

One near a brown-haired girl in the back, otherwise alone, gazing out the window.

Bellamy waved at the little boy with the stuffed dog as he passed, smiling and asking for its name. He bent down to get a better look, tilting his head when the boy didn't respond. He frowned, feeling the world tilt on its side for a single, nauseating second.

The boy turned in his direction, looking past him to the girl with her mother, just ahead. Bellamy turned, finding himself in direct view of the girl. The boy blinked, looking right through him.

Bellamy swallowed, stood. He took a breath in, released, feeling his fingers go numb. *Tap, tap.*

He turned back to the window, watching the shadows dance in the corner of his eye. Breathe in, breathe out. *Tap, scratch.*

'Hey!' Bellamy turned, chest tight. 'I saved you a seat,' the brown-haired girl said, smiling. She pat the empty seat beside her and turned back to the window.

He cast a glance behind him, half waiting for a monster to step out into the isle, claiming dominion over his nightmare. For a blackness to swarm, hungry in the way all starved things were. To consume. When nothing arrived, he abstained from clenching his jaw, cursing himself for wishing such an awful thing.

He took a seat cautiously, sinking down so slow he wondered if he might fall through into another world if he let himself rest.

When he didn't, he cleared his throat. 'I know you,' he said, before he thought better of it.
She turned to him, with a curve of her lips that whispered she knew every secret before he'd uttered it. 'You do?'

He nodded. 'You were. . .' he began. She was not so ghostly. She was real, concrete. She could see him. Spoke to him. She knew him, too. It was as if lifetimes of planning had led him here, to this moment in this dream, this world. Bellamy faltered, mouth open. 'I don't know your name.'

'But you know me?'

'I do.' He was certain. She smiled wider. 'Your name?' He asked, frowning.
She shook her head.

'Is it embarrassing?' He breathed a laugh to himself, 'it's okay,' ran a hand through his hair, 'my middle name is Bartholomew. It can't get much worse than that.'

She smiled wryly. 'It matters not what my name is,' she said, her words old and heavy. She was young, wearing a chunky brown sweater and her hair knotted from sticking her head out the window. But in that minute, she was archaic. Timeworn and venerable.

Absurd. Names were important. Valuable. Worth is not determined by what something is, but the weight you give it.

'Well,' he said, 'then I'll just have to give you one.'
She made a face at him, perhaps believing the idea was preposterous. As if she'd never had a name before. She smoothed down her hair with her hands.

Bellamy hummed, making a great show of thinking hard, glancing up at her to make sure she was paying attention. It struck him then, so dramatically he did not have to falsify his awe as the name came to him. He blinked up at her, stupefied, like he had just stumbled into Olympus on shoes made of wind.

'You are Loralai,' he said. 'Loralai, harbinger of shipwrecks.'

She cocked her head at him, thinking. 'Loralai,' she said, sounding out every syllable. '*Loralai.*'

Bellamy smiled, sticking out his hand. 'It is a pleasure to meet you, Loralai.'

She took it, an ancient amusement crinkling the corners of her eyes. 'It is a pleasure to meet you, too.'

III

A WARM, SALTY BREEZE DRIFTED over Bellamy's bare arms, blowing his hair into his eyes. He brushed it back, tucking it gently behind his ear.

Heavy waves lapped at the black, jagged rock he sat on top of, rain slicking its surface. Thunder rumbled overhead. Darkness pooled in its wake, thick enough he wondered if it was possible to leave a trail with his hand, should he reach up to touch it. Moonlight crested the waves, large and loud, endlessly crashing against each other, wild in the way that nothing tamed ever could be.

Lightning sounded far off, striking the sea and splintering. The ocean lit up beneath the crushing foam, glowing teal and green, luminescence fluttering, a heartbeat. Bellamy swiped at his forehead, slick with rain, and peered into the deep. Sailboats slipped over the waves, undeterred. Light shone over their sails. It highlighted one side of their silhouettes where tall men stood atop, facing inward and rigid. Lighting struck again, closer, lighting up the closest of the sailboats for an instant. The men atop remained cloaked in shadow.

Bellamy loosed a shaky breath, casting around for salvation. Thunder rumbled, low and heavy, lightningless. The sea churned beneath him speaking, warning. A single wave twice his height surged forward, stretching upward and scraping the moon.
It crashed down with lung-crushing force, swiping Bellamy down under the black waters.

The water beneath the surface was so cold it burned hot through his lungs, his eyes, his fingertips. Pressure bubbled up in his chest, fire behind his eyelids. Blackness creeped into the edges of his vision.

He swiped at the water with a clawed hand, useless, grappling for something solid amidst the water around him.

Moonlight filtered above the invisible tides above, around, taunting him with a light he could not reach.

Darkness licked at his ankles, swiping up against his skin, cool and inviting. He kicked at it, straining against the unseen current, and pushed to the surface.
He sucked in the night air in deeply, greed filling his lungs as he forced the water to leave him.

Another, smaller waved rushed over his head, filling his mouth with salt. Bellamy gagged as he surfaced again, shaking the hair out of his eyes wildly.

He spotted the rock he was perched on before and began to make his way back, fighting the waves the entire way. He swam directly against them, avoiding the temptation to let the hungry current swallow him whole.

The sharp, jagged rock bit the palm of his hand as he pulled himself up. The wind screamed against him, whipping his hair into his face, whining through the air like a lover.

He heaved himself over the flatted top, panting, and rolled onto his back, letting the rain hit his face and wash the salt away. Thunder rumbled hungrily and Bellamy opened his eyes. The dark clouds swirled above, ravenous and all-consuming, twining in and out from each other just as the waves lapping up at the jagged rock he lay on. A fork of light collided with the clouds somewhere above him, reflecting through whatever remained of the heavens. The sky flashed, on fire, glorious and destructive, burning as hot as the icy sea below.

Bellamy turned his head, looking back for the sailors on their small boats. The silhouette of one of the men turned to him, faceless. He swallowed as he sat upright, staring down the strange sailor. He felt its gaze bore into him, waiting. He turned to find the other sailors circling him, closer, feeling them regard him, eyeless as they were. Chilled rain soaked his clothes, and when the wind whipped against him, he shivered, unsure if it was from the cold. Bellamy sat up fully as the darkness of the night began to blur around him.

A large ship cut effortlessly through the waves toward him, driving with a questionable force. The harsh waves parted around it perhaps in memory of where the ship once was, where it may again be, the ocean itself was bending to the wooden skiff's will. The water below glowed a soft green. It pulsated lightly, thumping rhythmically, beating.

The ship slid closer, lining itself up to slip just beside the jagged rock Bellamy sat on top of. The sailboats drew inward, anger radiating off them. It caught in his chest and pulled, the violent feeling taking root inside him, curling around his veins, the fury his own.

A voice rang out clearly against the pounding of the storm, of his head. Bellamy looked up to the ship that had begun to pass, at the pure size of it as it drew nearer.

A familiar face stared back at him, amusement glittering across her features. Bellamy stood up, swiping at the hair that had begun to stick to his forehead again. 'Loralai?'

She smiled and stuck out her hand. A harbinger. The ship leaned over to accommodate, tipping, bending down so he could climb atop its shoulders.

Loralai stretched down over the railing, feet leaving the ground as she grasped for his hand. Bellamy stretched upward—farther than he considered he'd been able, took it, and began scaling up the side of the ship, her hand his grapnel. He flipped himself over the railing and landed on his back, panting. Coughed. Breathed with the belief that rest need be earned. He had merit. The rain slicked deck reverberated beneath him solidly. He felt each raindrop hit the deck like it had been his own skin.

Loralai loomed over top him, curious, then offered her hand again. He reached for it, and when their hands touched for the second time, he couldn't help but acknowledge how cold her fingers had been, in such a way that the storm around them had lived in her very bones, the wind her skin.

The gale whipped her hair, and for a flash, she was unearthly. Horrible, hands empty of a staff. The ship was her own. Her dark hair melded into the sky above, reminding him of a character in some great myth. Child of Darkness, Child of Night. Loralai gazed down at the dark waters below.

Bellamy turned about the deck, casting the idea from his mind. Large netting hung about each of the masts, the crow's nest high above. The darkness of the wooden deck was distinct against the quiet, green glow of the sea. The starch white sails stood proud against the harsh wind, direct in the way the ship was determined to sail, despite the opposing weather. With lightning uncomfortably close, the ship sailed on.

Thunder rumbled, the boat shifting as though the sea trembled with it. The ship held steady, perhaps itself unaware of the storm that lurked above, around, sinking into its own skin. Demanding to be seen in every way.

He turned back to Loralai, eyeing the way her dark, damp hair clung to her neck, the wet shine of her eyes, faced the sea and leaned himself gently over the rail. The sailors, still only illuminated by the moon, slunk back into the shadows beyond.

Bellamy clenched his injured hand, waited for the sharp bite, the crease of blood to drip down his fingers. Waited for the salt to sing piercing laments across his skin. A scar crossed his palm, healed and as old as he. He looked back to the rock he sat atop of, far on the horizon. The moon overhead stayed resolute.

Loralai sidled up beside him, leaning over the railing to look at the glow of the ocean, and then up again, searching for constellations in a starless sky. She turned to him, as if there was something cosmic to be found there, too.

He furrowed his brows and turned back to the ship, stalking off toward what he presumed to be the Captain's Quarters.

'Where are you going?' Loralai asked, jogging across the deck to catch him.

Bellamy shrugged. 'That's the point of exploring.'

He opened the first, large door, revealing a wooden desk littered with maps. Painted portraits lined the walls, faces smudged, suggesting the paint had never dried.

'I guess the captain's not home,' he said, stealing around to the other side of the desk and plopping down in the ornately carved chair. Loralai made a face at him. 'I guess that means I'm the captain, now.'

She huffed out a laugh. 'I don't think that's how that works.' He supposed she did not think it funny.

'Of course it is. How do you imagine anything begins, if someone first does not declare it?'

Loralai sat down in the less-grand chair, opposite him, and picked at the maps on the desk absently. 'You mean to say that everything must be imagined first? That nothing simply... *is?*'

Bellamy hummed, tossing his feet up on the other end of the desk. 'What is something if it is not named?'

She reflected thoughtfulness and turned her attention to the maps. She tugged one out from beneath the other and flipped it up in front of her, reading it like a newspaper.

'Well,' Bellamy said. 'Since I'm Captain, now,' he paused, and she looked up from the map. He took a heavily decorated coat off the rack and shrugged it over his arms. 'I think I ought to at least dress the part.'

Loralai offered a half smile. He considered it a win. 'If you're Captain,' she said, humour lighting its way into her tone, 'who's steering the ship?'

Bellamy's face fell before he shouted, 'Good Gods, the ship!' He raced out the door, turning in circles to find the wheel and rushing up to meet it, damning the way his hands fell against the wheel, meeting with a fervor and knowing they should have never left.

Loralai grinned beneath her hand, chest tight, and followed him out. He stood steadily at the wheel, contemplative as any true sailor.

'In my many years at sea,' he began when he knew she could hear, 'I have never seen a storm like this.'

Loralai looked at him, disbelieving. 'You're ridiculous,' she said, slightly awestruck.

Bellamy fought a smile as he turned to her, ever the stoic. 'You want to steer?'
She tried to deny him. 'I don't know how.'

He took ahold of her elbow, pulling her to the front of the wheel and positioning her hands before stepping away. 'I was at the helm once, before,' he said.
'You were?' She asked, confused.
'The captain of a ship my family and I were on once let me steer for a bit.'

She stared ahead blankly at the open waters. 'Then what happened?'

Bellamy furrowed his brows. He opened his mouth, then closed it. 'I don't,' he began, pausing. 'I don't know.'
The wind whipped forward again, the waves turning rough against the ship.

'I don't remember.' He took a step back, raking a hand through his hair.

The ground swayed beneath him for a single, dizzying instant. He looked up, watching as Loralai turned to him from the wheel.

He shook his head. 'This ship won't steer itself,' he said, gesturing to the wheel Loralai had left unattended. He shrugged off the captain's coat and draped it over her shoulders, distractedly.

Loralai made a face at him, and Bellamy raised a hand in mock salute. 'Captain Loralai,' he said, the picture of seriousness.

She blinked at him before tipping her head back and laughing. She covered her mouth to smother the sound, but it followed Bellamy into the darkness anyway.

IV

STARS LIT THE SKY, BURNING into the overwhelming blackness that encased him. The small campfire at the center glittered, hot and jealous, the cool evening's only reprieve. Embers drifted upward, melding into the heavens above. The moon sulked overhead, eye level with the horizon. Bellamy sucked in a deep breath.

Two children danced around the firepit, hollering things when another treaded too close, twirling about, giggling when they tumbled to the ground.

A bright light shimmered above, exploding midair and illuminating the Earth, casting Bellamy's shadow behind him. A commotion rang out as everyone came together, stomping down the fire and whispering like they might spook whatever was creeping within the flames.

Bellamy caught a face he knew across the pit and the mass of people around it, briefly catching her eyes. She disappeared behind the swarm of people and appeared beside him perhaps out of thin air. 'There you are,' she said lightly, a familiar warmth in her tone. Had he been invited? She seemed to have known exactly how he came to be here.

He made a face at her, wondering if his uncertainty made its way into the crease between his brows. 'Why wouldn't I?'

A single corner of her mouth lifted, as though he'd voiced the thought aloud.

Fire lit from behind the clouds, and for an instant, he had forgotten how to breathe. Starlight gleamed, hot and bright and huge, arching across the sky marvelously. It glimmered out, and the sky dissolved as if in Lethe. The darkness pulsed for a heartbeat, so deep it hummed; then it, too, faded.

Bellamy turned back to Loralai, face now illuminated only by the settling of the moon. It was brighter than it ought to have been. She gave a quick smile, then nodded upward. Another star streaked the sky and the air itself stood on edge, anticipating. It burned red, lighting the clearing so bright it could have been a second sun.

It fizzled out, and the world was again dark.

'A meteor shower?' Bellamy whispered.

She nodded back, eyes glued to the sky. Another star sang across the vast eve of twilight above them. Then another, impedingly closer in the open sky, grazing the Earth as close as it dared.

Once, he'd been made to read Icarus. He'd never been more envious of a star's ability to burn, and burn, and burn.

'Big stars,' he murmured.

Loralai nodded.

Another star crossed over their heads, golden and blazing and so large it took up nearly the entire sky.

Bellamy gave a small laugh to himself. 'Make a wish,' he muttered, turning in her direction.

She gave him a sideways look. 'Why?' She laughed, perhaps at the absurdity of his question.

'Wishes are important.' He turned back to the stars. 'It's good to know what you want.' The ground rumbled, deep and greedy. The smoking firepit wrought envy from its ashes, its embers.

Warm light bloomed behind them, soft and curious, licking upward at the blackness around. Bellamy turned, watching the small flame curl in on itself and stretch upward, unfurling smoothly.

It crept forward, spreading further into the dry grass before it doubled in size then shrank back down, appearing to balance on a highwire.

This, however, was not yet worse than the snapping of gum his father used to do.

He turned back to the audience, still gaping at the stars shooting across the sky. Another small fire stretched forward on the opposite side of the ring.

'Hey,' Bellamy said, panic soaking the edges of his thoughts. He turned to Loralai, still gazing at the sky.

'There's a fire.' The breath left his lungs, swallowed up by the rising flames. He fought the urge to choke down air by the mouthful.

She gave him a bittersweet smile, gesturing back to the stars that he was not looking at. Could not look at.

The flame sulked downward, laying out flat and joining in on the stargazing, a mere member of the reverie. Bellamy took a step back. He cast his gaze behind him, eyeing the flame on the other side of the ring, watching as it exercised its freedom in the dry, open field. Darkness fluttered around it, feeding the flame and all its light. It sank forward, bending over the length of the tall, dry grass blades. A lover, wishing worship. A god, keening for prayer.

Bellamy shout was soundless in the wake of the crackling fire.

The stars overhead whispered in a language he was incapable of understanding.

He looked back to the folks gathered around the circle, to the young woman with night-coloured hair, humming some sacred invocation to every star she was able to see. To the young boy clutching a yellowed, stuffed dog to his chest.

The fire reached forward, constant in its imperialism. He watched as the fire licked up toward his ankles, heatless. He looked to Loralai, who paid the growing fire no mind.

His attention turned back to the fire, and he didn't allow himself to think as he plunged his hand into the flames.

THE FIRE BURNED COLD AGAINST his skin with an ice so bitter it boiled his blood, his marrow. Bellamy snatched his hand back, cradling it to his chest. He'd heard once that the body was unable to remember pain. He hoped it held true.

Fate tempted his gaze as he forced himself to look, expecting charred skin, bloody and bubbling flesh stretched tight across his hand, melting and drooping away from the bone. His hand remained whole in the way it had been moments before. Only a single, thin scar marred his skin, cutting jaggedly across his palm.

He creased it with his thumb absentmindedly.

Bellamy looked back to Loralai, then to the fire, crouching down low, a whisper coiling on his tongue. It whirled one way, then another, speaking a language of movement and desire.

The darkness pulsated around it, thrumming down the sides of the flame, a constant other in the blaze. For an aching second, he could recall the way icy evenings might have once embraced him, gooseflesh rising to his skin, bringing salvation to its knees. Bellamy shuddered, baring his palms to the heatless flames for warmth.

Loralai called out to him, her voice echoing from somewhere far away. He turned, finding the fire engulfing the entire clearing surrounding him. It rose higher than any skyscraper he was powerless to have recalled, blending into the starlight, destructive in the way that all man-made things were.

She called his name again, urgency flooding her tone. He stood, pivoting on his heel, and resisted the urge to spring forward into the flame.

Fire hiked its way around him, circling, closing him in. He sucked in a breath and held it close.

The flames crackled audibly around him, popping embers in his direction as smoke flooded the air. Bellamy coughed, bringing his hand to his mouth, eyes stinging with tears.

He side-stepped the growing flames immediately in front of him and made his way to the other side, fire separating himself from the other spectators, now watching the flames with the same awe they had cast toward the sky.

Loralai met his gaze, urging him to run, to yield. To move.

He twisted in place, searching for an exit, finding that he was entirely encompassed in the flames that circled him.

She could have said his name, quiet beneath the loud crackling. He loosed the breath he'd been holding deep in his belly and took a step back, then another. He shook his arms out in front of him and launched forward.

Dawn inhaled, ready to strike the night sky with a greatness that would overtake it.

The horizon behind him lit pink as he jumped, hurtling himself over the flames. Ice curled inside his veins as he collided with the fire. Oblivion weaved its way into his vision and cradled him. Held him to its chest, because no time, no remarkable time had passed at all, and he was again a babe.

V

THE SUN GLIMPSED OVER THE tall trees, cold and isolated. The sky languidly turned pink overhead, and the fading dark lingered in appreciation. Heavy bass music bellowed across the air, loud and sudden, and the peace shattered into a thousand crystalline fragments.

Bellamy blinked hard, fought the urge to bring his hands to his ears as he spied a group of teenagers lean against an old, beat-up car. His gaze snagged on a dent in the frame on the far side.

The shortest of the group spoke, soft enough that his words didn't carry, and they all laughed. One by one, they all clambered inside the car. Its tan metal coating turned a soft rosy colour in the early morning light.

He squinted, eyeing the driver as he took a step in their direction. The boy that climbed into the passenger seat closed the door behind him and the light caught in the review mirror. Morning sun reflecting sharply into his eyes. Bellamy raised a hand to the reflection, again blinking hard as the driver stepped heavy on the pedal, the roar of the engine seeping through the ground. An odd intimacy wafted over top of him, settling heavy over the back of his neck, solid and firm, a reassuring hand. It rooted his legs in place as the car spun into motion.

It lapped around the parking lot of the school it had rested in, picking up speed at the corners. It turned sharply as it again neared the center, doing small, quick circles overtop the faded yellow lines. Bellamy smelled the hot rubber of the tires.

They rolled down the windows as they spun, tires leaving trail marks on the pavement, and the music came to him, louder. It was garbled under the base, familiar and heavy and utterly unintelligible. Bellamy took another step forward.

He raked a hand through his hair, ears ringing at the delighted shouts that sounded from inside the car. Laugher erupted again, louder than before. Mirth lit the air like the strike of a match, igniting a second so defined that there was no going back.

The car came to a sudden, screeching halt before it lapped again, oblivious to its sole audience member. It began again in the opposite direction. He laughed at the absurdity, humming along the tune that rumbled from the car, unplaceable. The vehicle came to a slow stop and one of the boys stepped out. A large, stupid grin stretched across his face as he stretched his fingers out wide before him. Bellamy squinted in his direction, almost recognizable, and took another step closer.

The car lapped the lot, coming back to the center where the boy stood, waiting, and spun tight circles around him. He tipped his head back and laughed.

Bellamy's fingers went cold, ice locking up the stretch between his bones and his skin. The car stopped short, drifting sideways when they'd decided the joke was over. The boy in the center remained uninjured, laughing harder than he had before. Perhaps denying death this way was humorous. To know that it reaches a bony hand for your throat, and to laugh when you deny even its grip. Perhaps it will remember this slight. Death knows all names, in the end.

He watched as someone clasped the boy on the arm, and the group again laughed. Harder, as if the whisper of death's hands on their throats made everything brighter.

He listened to the garbled choir that floated his way, swearing to no one that he knew them.

THE CAR STOOD RESOLUTE ON the opposite side of the lot, resting among a few others in a space lined in crackled yellow paint.

Long yellow buses began to pull in, lining up at the front of the building, the school standing imperial at the head of the lot. Other cars pulled in around him, turning off their headlights, unwilling to remove themselves from their vehicles into the cool morning air until at last the force became too great to ignore. They waited for a cosmic intervention to spring them into motion, or to give them leave. The air around him wet, its cool dampness reminding him of freshly pressed linens, folded neat and tucked away in the corners. He could smell his mother's soap.

The parking lot came to life seconds later, alive with attention as phantoms slipped across the lot, diving between the cars with steps so light they were near spectral in being, making up gods beneath their breath. A minute passed, two, and the lot was again a graveyard, void of bodies and ghosts alike, but mourning all the same.

A young girl stepped out of a parked car, the ignition turning off as she shut the door behind her. She tugged her long brown hair into a neat ponytail, waved when she caught his eye.

'Good morning,' she said. And for the first time, Bellamy noticed the sun yawning over the horizon, doing its morning stretches before it rose to meet the day.

'Morning,' he said by way of greeting, wonder filling the hollow space between his breath as he stared at the sky behind her. She gave him half a smile. 'Do you go here?' He gestured to the school.

The sky turned hot and red as the sun rose.

She smiled wider, as though she expected him to already know the answer. Confusion pinched between his brows as he turned back to the school. It sat shambled before him, broken and decrepit in a way that it had not been just before.

The windows were shattered. Each, individually. Ivy crept up its skin. It was more alive now than it could have ever been before. The lot around them was empty, devoid of everything besides that same, tan car in the far corner. Old, and covered in dust.

'Red sky in morning,' Loralai said under her breath. She drew her jacket tighter around her middle and zipped it up.

He looked back up to the hollow sky, hot and vibrant as the sun began to stand over the trees. 'Sailor's take warning,' he finished absentmindedly. Loralai looked up to him, brows knitting together. She tilted her head sideways, contemplative. He met her gaze and she looked away, shoving her hands in her pockets.

He stalked toward the car without casting her another glance, wiped the dust from its windows when he'd become close enough and peered through.

He swiped again at the glass with his sleeve, smearing away the grime, wiping away that thick coating of time. He tugged on the door handle, heaving against the heavy, rusted swing of its hinges. He looked up over the hood, and gave Loralai a quick, mischievous smile when he noticed her reluctance.

He slid into the passenger's side, rearing himself overtop the center console before he settled into the driver's seat of the car. Dust exploded as he flopped down into the frayed, faux leather of the seat. He coughed. Waved dust from the air as Loralai slid into the passenger seat, holding in a laugh. He swallowed deeply, laughed as she watched him draw it out. Her brows rose in disbelief.

Bellamy ran his hands down the wheel, finding the grooves worn in by time and patience, learned how his hands sat just right, resting the way old friends did. He jerked the wheel one way, tight in its age, and made loud, bubbling car noises as any child might have.

Loralai shot him a strange look, watching out the corner of her eye as he slammed his foot down on the gas. A getaway driver for the world's largest bank heist, a professional racecar driver. Someone who lived life fast.

She fought a smile and flipped down the visor, busied herself with her reflection, smoothed down her hair. He laughed like he'd told himself a joke, leaning back in the bare bones of the wearied seat.

He cut his gaze downward, mirth creasing the corners of his eyes, when he leaned sideways in his seat, reaching down to the floor, fingers grazing the tattered edges of the pedals. His arm burned as he stretched his fingers, grasping for something she couldn't see. He sat upright, the burn of his muscles forgotten—perhaps as though it was never there—and held up his catch, a fisherman reeling a particularly taught line.

Bellamy held a wallet out in front of him, the brown leather graying at its edges, and flipped it over, prying apart its folds. He shot Loralai a look that she pretended not to notice, leaning over the center console to garner a better view. He removed the driver's license, turned it over when he could not read the name, photo blurred, suggesting the cameraman sought to erase them entirely. The back was similar, warped and pale from years of heat and sun.

He peeled apart the bill pocket, pulling an old, assumingly out-of-date coupon for a small grocery chain from its thread barren leather folds. A dollar bill. A small handful of brown and silver coins. He counted the change

Loralai flipped the visor up and leaned back in the crackling pleather of the seat, bathing in the sunlight. She soaked up the amplified warmth of the sunrays that streamed undisturbed through the window.

'Hey!' Loralai cracked open an eye, unmoving. She feigned annoyance and turned slightly in his direction, enough to see him clearly. 'There's just enough change here for my favourite vending machine snack,' he said as he pinched the coins between his fingers, held them up triumphantly.

She quirked a brow, interested. 'What's that?'

He pondered for a minute, as though the thought had just escaped him. His face scrunched up, sour, before drawing completely blank. 'I don't know.' He felt a familiar cold snake its way down his spine, the tight grip on his bones, ice curling up the well-worn, taut marionette strings, invisible around his fingers.

The sun should have beat hot against his face, boiling in the old car, but ice made its home in his bones, so frigid it rendered him immobile.

The space in the car was too small.

Too cramped.

Too hot.

He remembered the hot summer heat from the windshield, how it choked out the air from inside him, as it should have now.

'I don't remember,' he whispered, dread pooling deep and heavy at the bottom of his stomach.

He remembered the weight of stones in his pockets, forcing him to the bottom of a lake. Surely, this is what drowning felt like.

He caught notice of a deep gash in the dashboard, the distinct urge to run his thumb across it coming entirely unbidden. Near overwhelming, absolving him of that damp pain that stuck to his bones. Before he could think otherwise, he'd done exactly that; felt the grooves in the old, dusty plastic in such a way that he was convinced he'd done it a thousand times before.

His hand drifted to the row of buttons at the bottom of the dash absent mindedly. He fiddled with them, pushing in one, and watching it pop out of place as he pushed in another. He pushed one rectangular button just higher. A cassette tape spit out, the writing faded as he took it into his hands. He flipped it over, the song list barely legible.

The words, individually, were ones he knew, but in no context he should have. Doodles in thick, black ink, grayed by time, surrounded the beaten lettering. He slipped it back into the player and snatched his hand back as the radio sprung to life.

The dash lit up, music springing from the blown-out speakers. Heavy guitar sunk into the old bones of the vehicle, quiet even as he turned the volume all the way up. He hummed along to the riff absentmindedly, fiddling with the unlabeled dials in a doomed attempt to clarify the sound.

It sputtered off, cutting out sharply as the radio turned off on its own. The rattling vibrations of the speakers washed away under the familiar tide of silence, settling back into its desolate, barren slumber. He pushed the button to eject the cassette again, but the car held it tight to its chest, reluctant to give up that hidden part of itself again. He pursed his lips as his fingers drummed against the steering wheel.

He reached across Loralai to open the glovebox in search of the vehicle's registration. It lay crumpled among empty boxes of other cassettes, their name's hand drawn, a collaboration of several people. Most of a food wrapper with a silly illustration. At least another dozen expired coupons.

Water bled the writing away, illegible. He crumpled it up into a tight ball and tossed it behind him, slammed the glovebox shut. Loralai watched him with rapt attention, head cocked at his growing frustration. He looked at her sideways, mouth drawn in a thin line, hating the way she looked at him now: explosive and frenzied.

As though he were about to blow.

He forced himself to look ahead into the yawning nothingness where the school should have been, was, only moments before. His vision simply stopped where the building ought to have been.

The dusty windshield he peered through was changed, fractured and spiderwebbing from a deep hole above the drivers' seat, not entirely unlike the moon in a sea of shattered stars. He sat back, leaning into the creak of the old seat, eyes widening at the violence that the car embodied. He wondered if the dash ever forgave it for the crumbling glitter that would never be removed, no matter how many times it was swept out.

The seats beneath them looked worm-eaten, old and phosphorous and devoured. Time had the ability to wear things away, but so did destruction. Perhaps they held hands here. Maybe that's what love was.

His legs were cramped in the compact where the pedals once were. There was a hole in the floor, and he could see the crepitate pavement beneath. The metal of the driver's door peeled away from its insides. The side of the vehicle had had caved in, crumbled beneath the weight of something heavy. His foot was stuck between its metal walls.

He leaned over the wheel, careful of his trapped foot, eyeing the hood of the car, shrunken up by force. It had been peeled away from the latch at the front, smashed in and destroyed. He nearly expected smoke to erupt from beneath the wicked metal confines, but it sat still, as though used to the damage.

The passenger seat remained mostly unscathed, despite the glass snow that had begun to fall from the shattered window. The contents of the car were upturned, tossed around in places that even he had not left them. His breath quickened, and the darkness pulsed around him in response.

It filled in the void beyond, answering. Perhaps he had called it. Perhaps this was mercy.

He smelled chemicals, sharp and strong.

Bright blues and reds flashed in his rearview mirror, and when he looked up to meet them, there was only the great darkness beyond.

He turned back to Loralai, choking away the feeling that had begun to rise in his throat, his chest. She watched him carefully, waiting for something. Anything, he imagined. Bellamy brought a hand to his head and winced.

A half-formed question bubbled to his lips when his hand drew away red.

Darkness crashed in with the refresh of a summer tide, cradling him from the miserable heat.

His heartbeat echoed audibly, and for an awful, fraction of a second, it is the best sound in the world.

VI

RAIN SPUN ITS WAY DOWN the twisted, red brick street, pooling in the divots in the road. Neon reflected in the puddles, scattered when fat raindrops rushed down to join them.

Bellamy bent down to peer at his own reflection, the puddle rippling as his figure came into view. A horn sounded ahead, sharp and loud, and he looked up. A car drove past, bouncing slightly over the uneven bricks.

A blonde-haired woman with a scar on her lip pushed passed him, flipping open her umbrella and walking swiftly over the loose sidewalk stones. Rain plopped down on his head, dripping down from a pipe above him. He looked up to meet it, fat drops landing on his cheek. He swiped them away and shook the hair from his eyes from where it clung to his forehead.

He stepped forward, continuing in the direction of the light-haired lady. He passed a shop with a large, clear window that displayed bright, colourful clothing. The lights flicked on as he passed, a bright, neon *Open!* beckoning him in. He eyed his reflection, face darkened too much by shadow to make out, and slicked back his hair, making faces that he couldn't see.

He turned back to the street, swiping the hair from his brow as it fell from how he'd styled it. A girl in a dinosaur tee-shirt toddled behind her grandmother on the other side of the street. Her powder-blue headscarf turned purple under the morning glow. She looked to his direction, and pointed a chubby finger at him. He gave his best smile, all teeth, even when she mentioned the models in the shop window behind him, the bright neon red against his back.

He frowned and turned further down the street.

'Hey,' a voice called out above him. He stopped, squinting up into the early morning light. Her hair fell smoothly over her shoulder in a loose braid as she tilted her head, blocking the pink sunlight streaming over the top of the building. Loralai smiled down at him from the first landing of the rickety metal stairway attached to the side of a building.

Bellamy smiled back and reached for the ladder, several feet off the ground. With a little effort, he hoisted himself up onto the first landing, ignoring the pitying look Loralai gave him as his hands went to his knees. He feigned exhaustion, breathing deep and heavy. Loralai made a face. He looked up through his brows at her, stopping his theatrics, a switch flipped, just to see if she was watching. 'I don't know if I can go on,' he said, smiling, 'I'm simply too tired, too exhausted.' He raised the back of his hand to his brow.

'Then I guess you won't get to see what's at the top.'

Bellamy opened one eye, squinting. 'The top?'

Loralai tilted her head to the side and spun on her heel to face the stairs, hand ghosting over the railing as she went up, up, up and did not look back.

Bellamy relented, and followed.

'I THOUGHT YOU SAID THERE was something at the top,' Bellamy queried, crossing his arms.

'I did not,' Loralai said, unbothered. 'I just said you wouldn't get to see it.'

Bellamy frowned again. A small radio sat on the corner of the roof of the building, straddling that endless fall and the immortality it would hold for those few seconds.

He strolled off in its direction, plucking it from its corner, teetering, and pressed in the sticky power button. The radio emitted sudden static, loud and abrasive. He jumped for the volume dial, turning it all the way down as he sat cross legged on the ground, fiddling for a working station.

Loralai took up the space beside him, sitting down and bringing her knees to her chest. She watched the pink clouds slink around the tall buildings, large glass windows reflecting soft oranges and pinks, the stars disappearing under the colour, quiet and tired. She rest her chin on her knees.

The radio tuned in to some classical station, the clearest he could find, and Bellamy turned up the volume, setting the radio down in front of the lip that surrounded the building roof. He remained standing and offered her a hand.

She took it, wary as he pulled her to her feet. He made an elaborate show of bowing at the waist. 'Care for a dance?' He asked, holding back a laugh.

She glanced between him and the delicate piano sounds drifting from the radio, soft under the quiet static. 'You dance?'

He stood, shrugging. 'My parents used to make me take ballroom dance classes.' Loralai stifled a laugh. 'My mom told me it would make me a heartbreaker.' Bellamy was holding in another laugh, too.

She made a face and took his hand.
He spun her once, she lifted herself onto her toes, throwing her arm outward in a dramatic flourish. She looked back to him and raised a brow. She twisted another way, laughing as Bellamy's eyes widened in panic. 'I don't know these steps,' he said.

She spun on her toes again. 'Do you need to?' She looked back to the radio. He tilted his head to the side and countered her step. Music spun around them, high and light and free.

Loralai made an effort to spin him. He ducked under her arm, laughing, and twirled himself. Sirens rang out in the street, blending in and out of the violin that sung to the piano. Loud, and growing. The sound swelled uncomfortably and Bellamy felt his hands rise to his ears.

The morning beyond was thick and infinite. Briefly, everything hung in balance.

No birds overhead, the radio muted, the sky bending down close, listening.

His shirt was too tight.

Rain began to drizzle above, quiet in the silent wake. The world went on.

Bellamy lowered his hands.

Loralai crouched beside him, eyes shining. She blinked, and it was gone. He looked at her, contemplative as she stood.

Loralai offered her hand. When he took it, the world disappeared.

VII

THE GREENHOUSE AHEAD WAS HALF sunken in the ground, ivy clawing its way up the fogged, broken windows. The way ahead was flat and even, the dirt path well maintained over time. Ice coated the grass blades, ground frozen solid, caught off-guard by the sudden cold. Bellamy picked his way forward and flattened his palm against the old glass door. Brushed his fingers against the broken edges of its centre. Frost coated the door frame, spreading just inside the doorway. He ducked under the top half of the glass door, suspended crudely by the frame.

A wall of hot air slammed into him, thick and tangible. He combed his fingers through his hair and stood on his toes, peering over the tall plant, rocking back onto his heels when he couldn't see more than just the ceiling above him. Sunlight streamed through the holes in the glass ceiling above.

He stepped around the tall plant, fingers trailing over the tall stalks of the stem that connected to the leaves, an icy white at their middle not unlike fireworks. He pinched a waxy leaf between his thumb and fore finger, drawing his thumb across the spider web of veins within it when movement caught his eye.

Just ahead, a figure ducked around the corner of a stone pillar, chiseling faded, worn by everyone before him who had traced its history with their hands.

He brought a hand to his brow, shielding himself from the sun and all its weight as he squinted in the direction the figure had disappeared off to. He picked his way through the sunken greenhouse, wary of the unevenness of the land, its eagerness to swallow the building up whole, reclaiming the space for what it could have once been. Distantly, he wondered if it would swallow him up, too.

Bellamy twisted around the column, pressing his back to it. It was easy for a childlike merriment to return to him, for him to again be a spy traipsing through lasers, space-age technology at his hip. He was unstoppable. A sunflower lifted its face to him in passing, feasibly tilting toward the sun, and looked at him with its gaze-less stare. And then, through him. Maybe the flower had never moved at all.

Someone with long, dark hair turned about just ahead, bending over a pot to reach another behind it, lifting a small watering can to its lip and watching it slowly drink in the world.

'Loralai?'

She turned. Smiled. 'Hello.' She pushed her hair over her shoulder and stalked toward him, setting the watering can down on a small shelf he had not noticed before.

'Where are we?' He asked, eyeing the strange livery that angled itself toward him no matter which direction he stepped.

'I believe it is called a greenhouse,' she said, a smile curling her lips.

He rolled his eyes. 'Never heard of it.'

Something scratched at the glass windows of the greenhouse on the far side, an awful whisper pulling chords deep within him. *Stay,* it whispered. It was very nice here.

'Does it matter?' She said, frowning.

He frowned too, not entirely sure what she was asking. 'I suppose not.'

The sun struck directly overhead, a few of the plants wilted in the heat, others rose to the challenge, soaking up everything the Earth gave them.

Bellamy felt no warmth on his skin, only remembering the far-off difference of the bitter bleakness that lurked just beyond the door. How bad would it be to stay here, where it was warm?

Here, where it was safe. Surely, whatever was out there was not in here. *Here,* where it was warm.

It must have been warm. It certainly could not have been cold. But then, he wasn't sure how cold was supposed to feel, either. He wasn't quite sure what anything felt like.

Something tapped on the glass, dragging their sharp nails and scratching the clear panes. *Tap, tap. Scratch.*

He looked to his right. To his left. He couldn't be sure. None of the windows appeared scathed. *Tap, scratch.* None of them.

Vines curled around the column in a way they had not been before. Stretching, reaching. Alert.

Alive.

Bellamy took a step back. Reached one hand out in its direction it before he thought the better of it and snatched it back.

'Have you never seen ivy before?'

He stretched his hand back out, tempting it with his touch as he neared the leaves that were pressed flat against the yellowed column, fanning themselves in the sun. 'Apparently not,' he said.

He pressed one finger to its central vine.

Two, as if feeling for a pulse. He turned back to her, gazing up at the other strange plants that hung down low from the ceiling, the way green moss crept in at every corner, stained and soaked and bloodied Earth pact in deep. Claiming, calling. Everything always returns.

'It's calm here.' He said, breathless, heart erratic. He felt needles prickle his head and he swore all the air had been sucked out of the room. And yet, he wasn't sure he could find it in him to care.

'Quite,' she said, brows knitting together. 'Why are you here?'

He turned back toward her, unsteady. 'However can you mean? Is it not enough that I simply *am* here?'

Her frown deepened. 'How did you get here?' She echoed, her tone firm in a way that he did not understand. A cloud passed overhead, and the greenhouse dimmed.

The greenery tucked into itself in the passing shade, hiding its face away until the light returned.

'I walked in through the door,' he said, feeling ridiculous. *Tap, tap. Scratch.*

'Before that.'

He sought again for the grating sound of nails on glass. All the panels remained as they had before. He thought hard, a headache creeping in. The clouds darkened further, stretching on above.

'I came from the path,' he said at last, recalling the frost outside. 'It was cold out.'

'It was?' Her brows lifted slightly in surprise.

'I think,' he said. Just in case he was mistaken. He couldn't remember it being cold, but surely if there was frost coating the ground, it must have been. What he really meant was that it was supposed to be cold. Just as it ought to have been warm inside the greenhouse. He brought his hands to his arms, crossing his chest and pretending to feel the heat on his skin *Tap, scratch.*

'Loralai,' he said, eyeing the greening walls. The plants looked up to him as he spoke, waiting for him to finally blink awake. 'Where are we?'

She made a face at him, opened her mouth and prepared to let her thoughts tumble out. Shut it. The plants looked on.

'Where am I?'

True horror was something inescapable, she decided. It was when you knew and decided you wanted to no longer. You cannot escape what already lives inside you, but maybe you could avoid it. Horror is the knowing, despite how you hide.

'You are in the greenhouse,' she said softly. 'My greenhouse.' The walls shuttered around them, a pane falling from the ceiling and shattering along the hard-packed earth like ice. Like frost coating the ground, glistening and shining and wet.

The walls that surrounded them breathed just as surely as he did, exhaling in every same way, pulse erratic and unstable and listening. The greenhouse was listening.

The ivy on the time-worn column tilted to him as he stepped away, pressing his back to it, raising a hand to his chest, to his head, through his hair.

Loralai took a step toward him. 'You were right,' she said, whispering. 'You are here.'

He looked to her as another tile fell, shattering along the ground. His brows pinched together at the crest of the. The far wall sank further into the Earth, stolen or reclaimed.

'It is enough.'

She looked at him in a way that he could not remember being seen. She looked at him with answers in her eyes, answers he did not know he so desperately wished for. Darkness taunted overhead.

'You are enough.'

The greenhouse slipped into the Earth.

VIII

BELLAMY BRUSHED HIS FINGERS OVER the too-tall wheat grasses, running his hands along their grainy stalks, watching them spring back upright upon release.

Dark brown fencing stretched over the hills, solid and wooden, damp where the late afternoon rain had soaked into its bones. It rolled over the ground, solidly resolute, guarding one stalk of grain from another, trailing all the way down as the tan stalks faded into taller, violet ones that blended up onto the distant mountains.

Bellamy touched two fingers to the fencing, dragging them down the rough grain, waiting for a splinter to nick its way under his skin. The earthy scent of rain wafted up to him as a breeze swept lazily through the air. He looked up into it, allowing it to run its fingers through his hair, bring that chilly pinkness to his cheeks, his mouth, waiting for the air to fill his lungs as it did just after he'd finished running.

The wind would not touch him so, despite how desperately he hoped it might.

The wheat stalks bent slightly in the wind, bowing low. It made him recall the giant scythes he'd seen in paintings in museums, held by a harbinger, a ruiner. Sometimes even Death himself.

But this place was deathless, he decided. There was nothing here that could be touched by awfulness. By terror or pain. By human hand. The fog around him swirled, craned inward to listen.

It swirled one way, and then another, until a familiar dark-haired figure stepped out of the mist, smoothing down her dark tresses. 'Hello,' she said.

'Hi.'

The mist stepped back, gave him space. The sun overhead should have been hot, boiling the mist away, letting the sogginess in the dirt rise. He had learned to be grateful for his shadow.

He cast a sideways glance at her, talking a step forward into the tall wheat stalks and parting them with his hand.

'Where are you going?' He heard her ask. He pushed his way forward, watching the ground refuse to be marked by his step, despite how soft it had been. Despite the rain that still curled away deep within.

'Does it matter?' He said absently. He wondered just how much truth was behind the sentiment.

She hummed playfully. 'How can you get to where you need to be if you don't know where you're going?'

He laughed and took hold of her wrist. 'Why do I need to be anywhere?' He tugged her along as he picked up speed, pushing his feet faster beneath him. She jerked along behind him as if she had never learned to move faster than she needed.

The wind whipped up around him as he ran, tearing heads from the golden wheat stalks, swirling them up into the sky and letting them glitter back down to the ground. The sun glanced off them through the misty clouds overhead, lighting them up bright enough that they seared like embers melting into the sky.

He laughed again, steering one way and then another, pushing through the wheat and winding them in circles. Loralai laughed too, voice light and nearly lost on the wind.

Bellamy pulled them to the line where too-tall lavender blooms stuck out of the ground. Dandelions puffed out of the ground, left of nothing but their small, wishful whisps. Both hollow and full, they stood waiting.

He took a deep breath. Rubbed his palms together. Glanced at Loralai, mischief alight in his eyes, and bound across the line. She looked at him like he'd just tracked mud across her clean carpets. Her brows pinched together, and much to Bellamy's confusion, she erupted into laughter. Loud and bright and bellyaching. Then he was laughing, too.

She swiped at her eyes. Blinked hard. He waved her over and before she could second guess it, she jumped across the line and landed solidly in the dirt, laughing again.

Bellamy laughed too, pointing a finger in her direction, and laughed soundlessly. She brushed her fingers against her cheeks and kicked a nearby puddle, watching the water arc upward and splash back down into the dirt. The rippling of the puddle left behind by her foot echoed, remembering.

He stepped forward, jumping up and slamming down into the puddle with all his weight, mustering as much force as he was able. Water splashed up onto Loralai's pantlegs, soaking in deep. She yelped at its coolness, then doubled over in laughter again.

Heavy clouds slipped overhead, twining above and wringing their hands. A breeze blew around them, whistling a tune he was sure he knew. He was positive of it.

Small lavender flowers caught in the wind, twirling in the air as the evening sun had begun to sink below the horizon. Had it really been so long?

'Loralai?' He wasn't sure why he said her name. Why the world had suddenly turned wrong. Why he was certain his heart should have been out of control.

Bellamy was unsure of many things. But there was no denying the lightning that beat the rain to the ground. The ire that lit up the very sky. He squeezed his eyes shut, as tight as he could will them.

'Over there,' she said quietly. He looked in the direction she was pointing, watching as the mist parted slowly around a white marbled building set into the base of the mountains ahead. She grabbed the wrist of his sleeve and tugged him on as the rain began to patter lightly down around them.

The sky turned a soft violet behind the clouds, and the wind blew the hair out of his face so he might see it. It curled around his face, the palm of a hand, holding his cheek lightly.

Loralai gave his sleeve a gentle tug, twirled him between the lavender sprigs. He laughed softly, the tension along his spine yielding. He looked up, watching as plump raindrops plopped down around him, on him. His cheek, his nose, rolling down over his chin as he spread his arms out wide to take it all in. The sky lit a deep plum colour beneath the gray clouds.

They stepped beneath a dark-wooded tree he had not seen before, pink leaves flitting overhead. Rain dribbled through the branches, dripping onto his soaked hair, rolling over his brow. Loralai reached up and plucked something from the tree and placed it into his palm. A cherry.

He plopped it into his mouth, pulling at the stem so only the fruit remained in his mouth, and bit down. He made a gagging sound, spitting out near the entire thing in search of the pit he'd neglected. Loralai barely smothered her snicker. He glared at her as she tried to wipe the look off her face and stuck the stem in his mouth, making a series of faces before pulling it back out, triumphant. He held it out in front of him, a knot in its middle. Loralai cocked her head to the side, perplexed. 'How did you do that?'

Bellamy looked at the knot in the stem. 'My. . .' he trailed off, uncertain. 'Someone.' He swallowed. 'Someone taught me how to do it.' He pocketed the stem. 'A long time ago, I think.'

'Why?' She plucked another cherry.

He shook his head. 'Does everything need a reason?'

Thunder rumbled through the ground, and the rain softened to a drizzle. She watched the troubled line between his brow form again before she made up her mind. 'Come on,' she said, nodding her head toward the mountains, hand open by her side. She curled her fingers, a weight missing. It was easy for him to imagine a pocket watch resting in her palm, ticking down toward something uncertain.

They stepped up to the marbled stairs of the pavilion, and Bellamy turned, seeing the cherry tree in the distance, sure that he couldn't have taken more than a few steps.

Wisteria hung from the marble ceiling, low and perfumed. The air smelled like rain and flowers and Earth. Petals fell from their stems and landed among his hair. He brought his hand to one of the low hanging stems and felt the butter-soft petals, the way they folded beneath his touch, breathed with the wind. He stepped to the edge of the railing and plucked stems of lavender, carrying handfuls of them back to the centre and sitting down. Loralai looked at him, puzzled.

He folded one stem over another, reached for a new one. Repeated. Loralai sat across from him, watching the way he tucked the stems together to make one long chain until he brought it back together to make a ring, using a final stem to tie it together neatly.

'How did you do that?' Loralai asked, unable to keep the awe out of her voice, suddenly aware of how frequently she would ask, if he gave her so many opportunities.

Bellamy looked up to her, snapping out of wherever he had gone. He picked up two new stems from the leftover pile and repeated the pattern slowly, watching as she slowly attempted at mimicking the chain. As she picked up a new strand and made neater folds. Again as she repeated the pattern, smoother, like she had been created with this simple knowledge.
She finished the chain, tying it off and tucking away her ends. Plopped it onto her own head.

'Now we match,' he said.

She made a face he did not know how to decipher. 'What was the point of this?' She took off her crown and held it out in front of her, contemplating if it had been weaved full of secrets instead of by her own hand.

'Does it need one?' He laughed. 'Not everything has importance,' he frowned, taking off his own crown. 'I think some things are simply meant to exist.'

He took apart his chain. Unfolded each of the sprigs. The sun sank lower on the horizon, willing the sky a deeper purple. He looked to her and offered a stem. 'Not everything needs exist for its purpose, I think.'

She frowned. Took the stem, twirling it between her fingers. 'Some things have value because we give it to them.'

IX

THE FORTUNA CIRCUS CAME INTO town every other year for only three nights. No one had ever seen them unpack. No one had ever seen them leave. It was as if they had simply appeared one night and were gone by that third sunrise.

Bellamy found himself tracing the metal arms of a carousel, rusted and enraged from being left behind. Roots grew over its gears, tying it down, holding it in place. Maybe it knew its mortality, in the way it could never be more than it is now. May never again be what it was.

Dusk ran her hands along its surface. A caress, a promise. A sprinkling of stars dusted themself across the opposite sky, a polar recognition of what it meant to be eternal. Bellamy looked up and made a short effort of counting them. The mechanical horses watched from their plastic boneyard with a reluctant contentment. The passage and the passenger, unable to tell who is meant to be who. Bellamy spun in a circle, gaze settling on a Ferris wheel settling back down on its haunches, exhausted after a lifetime of merriment, knowing nothing other than the weight of others touching the stars. A sigh escaped its hinges. Taunting, ready. Consumed.

He took to inspecting the things left behind in the seats close to the ground. A flower that may have been from a girl's hair, a small stash of arcade tickets. A hair tie in another. A roadmap with the names illegibly smudged. He snatched it up, unfolding the sticky pages, peeling their foreign histories apart. Ink stuck to the opposing side that made holes along its interior. He hummed, holding it up to the light and peering through the tears.

Loralai raised a brow at him through the hole. He hadn't heard her appear. He squinted at her and dropped the map at the sound of a bell, a whooping laugh, the joyous cry of a child. A dozen other sounds he did not know.

Warm globe lights were strung above him, crisscrossing from their strung posts, thrumming with electricity. Stars flitted overhead, jealous from the attention, turning away from the circus and all its inhabitants. The sky was tainted with that weary feeling, drained and beaten and tired after a long day when the weights are finally set down, when you can finally rest. Cast off your coat, your shoes, collapse into something other than yourself and forget how to be. But the Earth was solid beneath him, and the air was alive, and he had wanted nothing more than to forget how heavy the weights were. To cast himself into another delicious burden.

A small child ran by, fire in their hands. Prometheus was smiling, he felt. It sparkled and popped and fizzed, and the child—with hair much like his own—smiled, unafraid. Bellamy turned back to the carousel, just beginning the next ride, turning slowly in place. He stole a glance toward Loralai, who looked at him with equal amounts of mischief. 'Come on,' he said, volume lost on the shouting of nearby vendors hawking their contest, their prizes.

He took her by the wrist and jumped onto the spinning platform, trusting her to stick the landing as he began to weave throughout the metal steeds, sifting through them until he found one that suited him, had been waiting all this time. As if he were returning. He hopped onto its synthetic saddle, waiting for Loralai to catch up, her hands drifting over each of the horse's mane's as she passed. Paying a respect, a kindness.

'What is it?' He asked.

Loralai looked to him, a strange expression creasing her brow. She dismissed his question. He hopped down from the horse and turned to her fully. Someone shouted and he made a face of exaggerated shock before grabbing her wrist and tugging her along again, weaving through plastic shells and metal poles.

'What are you doing?' She said, half amused.

'We wouldn't want to be caught sneaking onto the ride,' he said, making a show of his empty hands, void of tickets.

Loralai opened her mouth, debating her answer. 'I don't think they were shouting at us,' she said, disbelief worming its way into her words.

He cast backward at her, making another face she was unsure of how to conduct. 'Yeah,' he said. 'But it's much more fun to pretend.'

LORALAI DRAGGED HIM ONTO SOMETHING evil.

It was the worst possible thing she could have chosen. He had been fine examining it from the ground. Admiring it, even. But to be at the top? Unacceptable.

Bellamy decided then that there was one thing he hated worse than gum snapping. Ferris wheels were the bane of his existence. Utterly and completely. They were evil. Perhaps she was too, for deciding this for him.

And yet, he was not angry, with the heavens in reach. Maybe this was what people meant when they said to reach for the stars. To stretch out a hand and wish, to reach out and take something, to hope, to cut a piece of the sky for yourself when your prayers went unheard.

The stars whispered something in a language he did not speak; ancient and forbidden and tempting, scratching at the back of his mind. Stars were not meant for taking. They would burn up in your hands, taking your skin with it, marring your bone. Better to look at them from a safe distance, shield your eyes when they're close. Stars were made for easy wishes, when you could look at them straight on and know that you will not be blinded for it. Stars were ghosts, and they knew what it was live to live once, too.

Bellamy reached out and traced the sky anyway, waiting to see if he might feel the stars, jagged against his fingertips, rough and hot in his palm. He did not.

Loralai stood in the tiny carriage that they'd snuck into, leaning onto the railing with her elbows, uncaring of the way the cart rocked. For the first time, Bellamy was helpless to the heady, powerful feeling the height gave.

He looked above the trees, felt the wind cut through him, knowing exactly which ways to cleave around his bones, his skin.

The Ferris wheel groaned to a halt as they reached the top, metal gears sticking in place. The moon overhead dawned a smooth, silvery crescent. Thin and waiting to be plucked. A sickle, waiting to yield harvest.

He thought of the wheat fields his grandfather used to tend, a giant red tractor that was older than even him. The apple orchards they visited every autumn, his mother's favourite flower that bloomed in the under the moonlight. The smell of pine. A scholarship, a graduation.

'What are you thinking of?' Loralai said softly, face bathed in luminescence.

Bellamy turned to her absently, half a smile on his lips. 'I was just remembering. . .' His face morphed into concentration. She pulled her hair over one shoulder neatly and rest her chin on her fist, elbow molded to the metal bar of the car.

He swallowed, feeling the stars pulse above him in anticipation. They thumped readily. A warning, a heartbeat. Fireworks yawned upwards, whistling.

'I was remembering my grandfather's wheat fields,' he said finally, quietly. 'And the hikes my brother and I used to go on together.'

The sky erupted in colour, making even the stars jealous. Not everything is meant to be gentle.

He felt the shake of it down in his very bones. He was certain purples and blues lived there, now. Deep beneath his flesh. Maybe that was a way of living, too.

Loralai's face softened as she waited for something to collapse, to break. The world is not so fragile, he knew. 'We should go on more of them,' he whispered, uncertain. As though, if he'd said them too loudly, the world would swoop down and take them back.

'That would be nice,' she said, taking a seat opposite him, unconvinced.

Another firework shot into the sky, casting the sky in purples in blues, brighter and closer than any star.

'My mother used to take me to the Fortuna Carnival.'

Loralai gave a small smile. 'Really?'

He nodded, returning the gesture. 'She used to play the games until she won a prize from each of them. Like it was a contest. She was really good at the ones with darts. I think that was why my father liked her.' Loralai smiled wider. 'She died a couple of years ago. I haven't been, since.'

'Do you regret it?' She asked, so quietly that for a moment Bellamy wondered if she'd really said it at all.

His brows pinched together. 'I don't see the point. Regret doesn't change what's already happened.' He moved to the other side of the cart, peering down over the rest of the carnival. A young boy hung off his mother's leg, twirling around her arm by the grip of her hand, a balloon in his other.

'I think I've forgotten a lot of things,' he said. 'A lot of useless, important things.'

Loralai cocked her head quizzically. 'What do you mean?'

He made an effort to brush off the chill that coated his arms. 'Things, details. They're not important. They don't add any more meaning than excluding them does.' He swallowed. 'But they're important to me. To someone. That's enough, isn't it?'

Loralai huffed a laugh that held no amusement. 'I think it is. Just because something isn't important does not mean it has no value.'

She took up the small space beside him.

He nodded, content as the darkness pressed in overhead.

He raised a mock glass in salute. 'To value,' he said.

Loralai laughed. Copied the movement.

'To value.'

X

BELLAMY MADE WARMTH BETWEEN HIS hands, watching his breath puff misty clouds in front of him. The wooden seat beneath him was hard, and his dark, black sweater did nothing to warm him. He wasn't sure he'd ever been so cold.

He caught the shine of his dress shoes, neat and polished. He couldn't recall changing into them. He brought his hands down to his lap, thumb rubbing gently over the scar on his palm, jagged and rough.

Loralai stole into the seat next to him, angling them so they were separate from the rest of the congregation as they filed into the small church.

Sunlight streamed through the tall windows, warm sunbeams casting patterns and rainbows on the floor. It reminded him of the light on a forest floor, patterned from the leaves overhead, of how much he wished to step between their cracks and fall. And fall.

Bellamy contemplated, a headache forming between his eyes. 'Whose funeral is this,' he whispered, unsure if it was truly a question. She shook her head. 'Loralai?'

She hushed him gently. He looked around, at all the faces he should have known. Stood, and made his way to the casket at the head of the pulpit. Waited behind a young boy and his mother, whispering words that ought to have made sense.

Watched as they stepped away, as he looked at him. Through him. Bellamy shivered and took a step around a man with mussed hair and ink-stained hands.

Cast his gaze into the still body that lie beneath the dense wood, holding and carrying. At the young boy and his dark, floppy hair, a scar on his lip, his palm. A small sprig of wisteria melded between his closed hands.

The world was too bright, he decided. The sunlight was startling. Wrong.

His breath caught in his throat and, despite himself, he let it.

Loralai crouched in front of him, solid among the ghosts surrounding them. His knees buckled, and he hit the ground to meet her. Let his breath escape him in totality. Exhaled again until there was nothing left inside, wishing for the burning feeling to return. That hot suffocation that settled between his ribs until his fingers went cold. His fingers were already cold.

His hands were ice.

He squeezed his eyes shut, willing the hot tears that had begun to pool in his vision away, watching distantly as they hit the carpet of the church floor. He stood, rage flooding his veins, hot and welcomed. Stormed off down the aisle.

'Bellamy,' she called after him. 'Wait.'

He paused, reeling. Spun on his heel and took two large steps toward her, meeting at the centre, the ground spinning dizzying circles beneath them. The air was taught between his damp palms.

'I never told you my name.'

He couldn't read her face, thinking her undeterred. 'No, you didn't.' He blinked and swore that it had been snowing inside the church.

Noticed that they were the only ones left inside. His breath floated in front of him. He looked to the window. Then out.

Stepped around the wooden church pews. Stretched onto his toes to peer out the window like he had when he was a child. As if he were no longer. The floorboards creaked heavily beneath his feet, the carpet peeling away from the wall, riddled with time. Grime coated the far wall; the stain of the ceiling had spread. Mold crept its way onto the window frame. He did not care.

A group of people were gathered around just outside the small plot of land. At once he was young again, wandering off into the woods. He was old, burying his wife. He was lost, burying a child.

He was not a child.

Bellamy stumbled into the winter chill, the wind whistling through the bare trees mimicking sirens, loud and uncaring who they startle. The noise was here to stay.

Could he say the same?

The ground was frozen beneath him, hard and unmoving under his weight.

Loralai came beside him, standing far enough away that he was unable to swat at her. He lowered himself to the ground again, forehead hitting the frost-covered grass. A train horn sounded in the distance, smoke puffing over the pine trees.

The sun sat high overhead. Had it not just been morning?

Bellamy brought his hands to his head and covered his ears.

'Bellamy,' Loralai said softly, breaking through the fog in his head. 'Bellamy you have to stand, now.' Her calmness was overwhelming. Contagious, even.

His fury no longer seemed so important. He was empty, anyways. Drained from all that had been. He should have been angry. Livid.

He was not.

The world swayed beneath him as he got to one knee, then another. Stood slowly. Up and up and up until he was certain he was floating. His shoes shined beneath him in the cold, daring him to test their genuinity. He had been a spiteful person, once.

Now, he thought himself spent.

He pushed his way through the small crowd of people, gathered outside, catching glimpses of conversation.

Unfortunate. . .

'...And the way it happened, too.

He swallowed.

At least. . . other boys survived. . . heard anything from their parents?

He balled his hands into fists at his side. Released them.

Had his whole life been summed up into *unfortunate?*

A car wreck, of all things, someone said. He turned to the direction he caught wind of it in, unable to tell who had said the words, words that he surely should not recognize. *Could he have been any more stupid? He put all their lives in danger.*

He gripped the hem of his sweater, shoved his hands in his pockets. It took everything in him not to scream. He was sure that no one would hear it anyway. What would have been the point, then?

Insanity was a curious thing, he figured. To be here and somewhere else entirely. Haunting yourself so clearly that you are your own spectre in a life you might have lived. In a world that you may have known. Could it be so simple? To be both afraid of the dark and to be the thing inside it?

Loralai stepped up beside him. Perhaps she was a spectre, too. He blew out a breath. 'Who are you?'

She exhaled, watched as the snow fell into her palms. Melted. He'd never been so jealous.

'My name is Loralai,' she said, cupping her hands together. 'You gave me that.'

He looked to her, confusion rippling across his face. 'I was not lying, on the train,' she said simply. 'I did not have a name, before you gave me one. No one had ever bothered to do that.'

He bared his teeth. 'Well, now you're the one with a name.' He felt the heat rise to his cheeks. Should have been glad for it, but it only drove him further. 'May everyone use it but you.'

She raised her gaze to him. 'You know what I am, Bellamy. You always have.'

He let the tension fall from his body. Hung his head. Turned back to the group of mourners gathered in the field.

'I'd never been given flowers before,' he said.

She put a hand on his shoulder. 'You deserved to be loved like this when you were alive.'

He thought of a thousand things he wished he could've said, might've howled to the wind, to the sky. He wasn't sure if they'd listen.

'I graduated four months ago,' he said, turning his head in her direction. 'My life was just getting started.'
Her words were thick with a strange emotion when she spoke. 'Your life is over.'

Wind sliced through him, and as he looked back to the group in the field, they were gone.

He stepped to the stone they left behind, his name carved deep within. *Set in stone,* he laughed. Loud enough to compete with the winter wind.

Stupid. It was stupid.

All of it.

He never should have gotten into that car.

Loralai's question echoed in his head. *Do you regret it?*

He swallowed. 'I regret it,' he said to no one but himself.

She took a seat in the snow beside his headstone, taunting the frost. 'Aren't you cold?'

'I am unfeeling,' she said. Looked away. 'I was, until you wandered through that gate.' He frowned at her and took a seat. 'I thought people were silly. Worrying about silly made up things.' She smiled in a way that was both more and less. 'They mattered to you. You made them matter.' She put a hand to her chest where her heart might have been. For a moment, she looked as if she were counting a pulse. 'There are no rules when you play your own game.'
A moment passed. Two. He supposed time did not matter anymore.

'I'm not ready,' he said, voice wavering only a little.

She gave him a look that for once, he knew. He'd given it to her many times. 'No one ever is.'
She stood. Offered him her hand.

He knew little of the version of the world he'd come to wander among, but he knew that this time, when he took her hand, there would be no coming back.

He stood.

Looked down the headstone. The word below his name.

Valorem.

Bellamy smiled to himself, and took the Reaper's hand.

ADDENDUM

DAWN STRETCHED ACROSS THE SKY, clawing at the dusk, knowing they may never touch. Yearning was special that way.

A girl with dark auburn hair sat alone in a train car, braiding her untamed hair back out of her face. She smoothed it down one way, produced a hair tie from her pocket and tied off the ends.

Caught a glimpse of her reflection in the window. Untied her hair and ran her fingers through it. Some things were meant to be wild.

Something dark tapped across the glass of the window, scratching down the panes.

Finally, she pushed open the frame, letting it in.

It hummed at her as Darkness filled the cabin.

How curious, it said, speaking into her mind. *Your heart, it beats.*

She bit back a remark, remembering the strange feeling of the rain on her skin. The weight of a ship beneath her palms. A dozen lost conversations.

A heart is just a thing, she said, wondering if she misunderstood.

The Darkness hummed to her, picking at the lawlessness of her hair. *And yet, it beats.* She shook her head. *You mourn.*

I do no such thing, she said. I am Death.

The Darkness chuckled. That was not always your name. But now, you have earned another.

She ignored it, stepping off from the train as it came to a rest, settling back onto its hinges, steam puffing high above. She sat down at a piano bench as it appeared before her, waiting, fingers resting indecisively over the keys. The Darkness shrouded around her as if clasping her on the shoulders.

She felt it smile against her cheek, doubtless that it had won more than just an argument. *There is a difference in who we are and who we've left behind,* she said as she began to tap out a tune.

And have you? It spoke. Left him behind?

Her head shot up. *He is gone,* she said, determined. *But he will live forever, too.* The Darkness chastised her this once. *To be deathless is to defy death.*

An end is not simply so.

67

I CANNOT SCORE AN ENDING WHEN
THERE MAY NEVER TRULY BE ONE.

Ashton Morgan

Lend Me Your Eyes